All Dogs Go To Heaven 2 ™

A novelization by Ron Fontes and Justine Korman
Based on the story by Mark Young & Kelly Ward
and the screenplay by Arne Olsen and
Kelly Ward & Mark Young

Troll

Special thanks to Susan Christison Toumaian, Eric Stein, and Sylvia Graham.

Chapter 1

Charlie B. Barkin was bored. He mumbled to his old enemy, Carface Caruthers, "Only in heaven can a bunch of squeaky-clean angels get awards for being extra squeaky clean."

Charlie scanned the horizon. Fluffy white clouds formed beautiful pine trees, mountains, and fields. No matter which way he turned, Charlie saw the same peaceful scene. The handsome German shepherd stood in a crowd of dog angels watching Angel Anabelle bestow awards to hounds with halos. Each honoree was given a diamond-studded angel-wings pin.

Charlie knew he would never get one of those. He wasn't a bad dog, but he just couldn't be, well, *good* like these other goody-two-shoes. Heaven was a little too sugary for his taste. Where were the garbage cans, the action, the alleys, the party music? Here all you ever heard was Angel Gabriel's horn. Its music was pretty, but it didn't make you want to howl.

Charlie was almost glad that Carface had shown up in heaven. Things had been even more boring before the bulldog's arrival. The last time Charlie had seen Carface on earth, the bulldog was being chased by a giant alligator. Maybe that's how Carface met his end. But nobody talked about stuff like that in heaven. It wasn't polite. Everybody was polite in heaven—and neat and clean and proper.

Anabelle pinned glittering first-class angel wings on a proud springer spaniel. "And that brings us to our final honoree . . ."

Anabelle was a pretty whippet, but Charlie was still bored. "Now I know why they call this eternity. Everything here takes forever."

"*Shh!*" Carface shushed with one paw held up to his flat, bulldog's muzzle. Back on earth Carface had been a crook. He liked to think of himself as a hotshot, always finding an angle.

Carface was the dog who framed Charlie and got the innocent shepherd sent to the pound.

When Charlie escaped to nail the real killer, Carface had Charlie run over by a car. Then he tried to use a little human girl named Anne Marie to cheat at the races. The bulldog had been thoroughly rotten. He wasn't the least bit good or loyal or kind, the reasons all dogs go to heaven. But since rules are rules, even cruel Carface was as welcomed as any other dog.

Charlie couldn't understand what was going on. Lately Carface had been acting like a model angel. Maybe heaven really changed a dog. But if it changed somebody as mean and mangy as Carface, why didn't Charlie feel like he belonged? At least Charlie knew that no matter how many halos Carface polished, the bulldog would never make first class.

"I'd like to see them try to give *me* one of those merit badges," Charlie said. Other angels shushed him.

"Where are your manners?" Carface asked.

Charlie scoffed. "Manners? This from a guy who can't eat without getting food up his nose!"

Anabelle continued, " . . . for making the most of what he has to work with: Carface Caruthers."

Charlie's jaw dropped open. *What was this?*

Carface said solemnly, "Remember, Charlie,

it never hurts to play the game." The bulldog's jowls lifted in a wide grin. He trotted up to the awards platform. Charlie thought the bulldog looked like a crooked politician.

Anabelle reached up to pin wings on the big bulldog. "I only hope that our other angels, who have yet to distinguish themselves, soon follow your shining example."

As the dogs politely applauded, Charlie felt everyone staring at him. Now he was the only dog without first-class angel wings. Even *Carface* had his wings! When Carface returned to his place, Charlie grumbled, "Halo polisher."

Then Charlie's ears perked up as a wonderful golden tune filled the air. The trumpet of the Angel Gabriel was opening heaven's Pearly Gates to welcome newcomer angels.

"Whoa, I'm late!" Charlie exclaimed. He jostled through the orderly ranks of angel dogs, leaving a ruckus in his wake. Anabelle shook her head and sighed. Charlie was such a rowdy dog.

Gabriel's tune was fading by the time Charlie reached the Pearly Gates. Gabriel had placed his golden trumpet on a marble altar. A glass bell jar lowered itself neatly over the magical horn. Gabriel's horn still hummed with a constant sweet note only angels could hear.

Charlie skidded into a small gathering of angel dogs. They toppled like bowling pins.

"Hey, watch it," a big white Samoyed barked.

Charlie raised his paws. "Sorry, lousy brake pads. Have the newcomers touched down yet?"

Clouds swirled and opened around a glowing tunnel of light. With a roaring *whoosh,* several dogs flew through the tunnel to land on a cloud platform just inside the Pearly Gates. A fat dachshund plopped right on top of Charlie! The German shepherd sank into the misty clouds under his paws. Charlie thought this was a *fine* way for an old pal to treat someone who came to greet him.

Itchy, the dachshund, looked around. The only thing that seemed familiar was the chicken bone clutched in his chubby paw. "Where am I?" he wondered.

Charlie poked his head through the puffy whiteness and said, "Itchy, you old dachshund you!"

Itchy could hardly believe his eyes. "Charlie?"

Charlie took the chicken leg and inhaled its savory aroma. "Gee, Itch, you shouldn't have."

Itchy scratched himself in confusion. "Charlie, is that you? It *is* you! Hey, wait a minute. Aren't you . . . d-d-dead?"

"As a dog who eats chicken bones," Charlie teased.

He was just about to pop the chicken leg in his mouth when an angel official whisked away the leg. "Sorry sir," said the official. "You can't take it with you."

Itchy patted his own furry body as his mind slowly added two and two. "So that means I'm . . ."

Charlie raised his paws, and a spinning gold halo appeared. He set the halo over his old friend's head and said, "Welcome to paradise, Itch."

The beautiful horn sounded again. The gates swung shut. The angels and newcomers walked away, raising little puffs of cloud.

Carface stepped from behind a fluffy pillar. He smiled like an angel, but little devils danced in his eyes. His smile was as false as it had been at the awards ceremony. Carface was still Carface, and he'd just found the perfect angle. He'd hooked up with a real hotshot. The dope trusted Carface, and Carface planned to use that trust to take the hotshot's place. Maybe Carface could take over the hotshot's whole operation! But first, he had to pull a job.

Carface slipped under the velvet rope that

ringed the marble altar. The bulldog thought this job was too easy, like taking candy from a baby. All these goody-goody angels were so honest, there were no alarms. Carface greedily rubbed his paws, then reached to remove the glass bell jar.

Unfortunately, the glass wouldn't budge an inch.

Then Carface had another idea. He unpinned his first-class angel wings and approached the bell jar again. The glass squealed as he drew a circle with the diamond wings. He reached through the neat hole and grabbed Gabriel's horn. Carface casually tossed away his wings as he scurried to the Pearly Gates.

The bulldog put Gabriel's horn to his flat face. He blew a feeble bleat. The gates quivered.

Carface took a deep breath and tried again. This time a sour *blat* opened the gates a little bit.

The stubborn bulldog tried again and again, until his fat cheeks were sore. Finally he managed a long, low *mooooaannn* on the trumpet. Wedging his halo between the gates, Carface squeezed through the crack.

Carface ran to the edge of the clouds. He grinned as he looked at the horn. "Baby, you're my ticket to fame and fortune!"

Then something happened that wasn't part

of Carface's big plan. As Carface bent over to remove his angel's gown, he accidentally bumped the horn off the cloud!

Carface grabbed at the golden trumpet as it fell toward San Francisco far below. But his paws touched only air.

Carface had to get that horn back. He desperately dove over the edge after the horn. Unfortunately the horn got away from him and fell down to earth.

Itchy soon discovered he didn't itch in heaven. For the first time he could remember, he didn't have the urge to scratch at all. He'd never felt like this before!

"This is heaven, Itch, fleas go to . . . the other place," Charlie explained.

Itchy was amazed. Anything he wanted was right there! The streets were lined with fancy dog houses and silver bowls piled high with juicy bones. There were peaceful courtyards where angel dogs polished their halos. Heavenly choirs sang beautiful music. A pretty poodle plucked a golden harp. Two angel dogs flew overhead.

"Wow!" Itchy cried. "Can everybody fly here?"

Charlie nodded. "All part of the basic package."

"I'm going to like this place," Itchy declared.

"Believe me, it gets old fast," Charlie said. "It's just too blissful. All the hallelujahs and hosannas will drive you bananas. Every day feels like a year."

Charlie explained to Itchy, "The flying and all the free food might be great for you. But for me *there's still something missing.*"

Itchy looked up and saw the firmly closed Pearly Gates towering over the heavenly landscape. He liked what he saw. "You might want to rethink this," he told Charlie.

Just then a shimmering sphere of rainbow light floated down. The light faded, and Anabelle stood in its place. She said, "Gabriel's horn has fallen from heaven and landed on earth, in the heart of San Francisco."

"Without the horn, the Pearly Gates can't be opened!" a St. Bernard exclaimed.

Reginald, a Welsh corgi, said, "Then no more dogs will get into heaven."

"Lucky dogs." Charlie nudged his friend.

"Reginald, I'd like you to go back to earth to retrieve the horn," Anabelle announced.

Charlie's ear's perked up. "We can go back?"

Before Reginald could answer, Charlie elbowed his way through the crowd to the pretty whippet.

"You can't send Reggie," he told Anabelle. "Down there, they got rats bigger than him. You need someone who can zip down and back before big Gabe finds his horn missing. Someone who knows the ropes and the dopes. Someone who's . . ."

". . . just like you," Anabelle concluded.

"I don't know. I'll have to check with my people and get back to you," Charlie said artfully. "*Ohhh*, I've got to earn my wings somehow," he said as he polished Anabelle's first-class pin. "What the heck, I'll do it!"

Charlie turned to go. Anabelle grabbed his halo. "Hold it! To find the horn, follow your ears. It gives off a steady heavenly tone that only angels can hear."

"Only angels—got it." Charlie was restless; he couldn't wait to get back to earth!

But Anabelle had more instructions. She granted him one miracle to be used only in an emergency. "This is serious, Charles. If the horn falls into the wrong hands, it could mean disaster for us all."

"You can count on *Charles*," Charlie agreed hastily.

"I know, because I'm sending Itchy along to keep you in line," Anabelle said.

"But I just got here!" Itchy cried. "I have flying lessons after lunch!"

With a wave of Anabelle's paw, the clouds around Charlie and Itchy rose into a swirling funnel. The dogs were whisked down. Anabelle called after them. "Bring back the horn, Charles. Otherwise there will be heaven to pay!"

She could hear Charlie say, "Got it!"

Chapter 2

It was midnight in San Francisco. So no one saw the white tornado spin down out of the sky. And no one saw the two dogs that appeared when the funnel vanished.

Itchy felt dizzy. He wobbled on his short legs.

Charlie didn't notice he was dizzy. He was too happy to be back. "Trash! Exhaust fumes! Graffiti! We're home!"

Both dogs jumped when they heard the squeal of cable car wheels. One of San Francisco's famous cable cars came up over the hill behind them. Itchy and Charlie watched the car pass.

Charlie smelled double-chili cheeseburgers with onions and pickles. His mouth watered. Charlie went to get a burger, but Itchy held him back.

"No, Charlie! First we find Gabriel's horn, then it's straight back to heaven."

"What's the hurry? Let's have some fun," Charlie urged. He heard music—and it wasn't a heavenly harp!

Charlie chased the guitar's wild wail to a dog restaurant tucked away in an alley. The banner over the stage announced a talent contest. At the moment there wasn't much talent on display. The country-western singer was way off-key. But Charlie didn't mind. It was exciting!

Dogs played cards at some of the tables. Others were eating luscious-looking junk food. It smelled so good! Charlie thought the best way to start his evening was to get a big cold root beer. He barked to the bartender, "How about a frosty one for the Chuckmeister?"

The bartender didn't respond. He passed a mug of soda right through Charlie!

Charlie was amazed. "What?"

"We're ghosts!" Itchy exclaimed.

Charlie looked in a wall mirror. He saw the

dogs playing poker behind him. He had no reflection!

"Anabelle! Of all the rotten tricks," Charlie moaned. He was back on earth, but he couldn't do anything except watch other dogs eat and play cards . . . and have fun.

Just then the country-western singer finished his act. The spotlight fell on a stunning Irish setter.

The master of ceremonies, a slick Labrador, leaned over a microphone. "Let's have a warm round of applause for our next contestant, Miss Sasha LaFleur."

Now Charlie was *really* unhappy that he was only a ghost. This was the most beautiful dog he had ever seen. Every dog in the place had his tongue hanging out.

"Itch, my heart is beating a million miles an hour. I can hardly breathe," Charlie gasped.

Itchy considered this. "Maybe it was the change in altitude. My ears popped. Did your ears pop?" he asked.

"Now I know what was missing in heaven," Charlie said without taking his eyes off Sasha. "I've got to meet her!"

"But she can't even see you. You're an angel," Itchy reminded his friend.

"Quit reminding me!" Charlie barked.

"Back in circulation, eh, Charlie?" a familiar gravelly voice said.

But Charlie wasn't paying attention to anything, except the slinky setter. "My circulation's fine," he said dreamily. Then he suddenly realized whose voice he'd just heard. "Carface!"

The bulldog jumped down from the motorcycle sidecar he'd been sitting in. "I heard you was in the neighborhood."

"Oh, yeah. I got time off for good behavior, but what are you doing here?" Charlie wondered.

"Missionary work." Carface tried to look angelic. Then a rat waitress passed with a box of cigars, and the bulldog said, "I'll take one of them."

Charlie chuckled. "She can't hear you."

"Two bits, Carface," the waitress said. She handed a cigar to the bulldog.

"Put it on my tab," Carface said.

Charlie and Itchy were stunned. How could this be?

Carface knew what they were thinking. He tapped the collar around his neck. "As long as I'm wearing this collar, I'm flesh and blood."

Charlie's eyes grew big. This was his chance to stay! He forgot all about Gabriel's horn. He was going to party with that pretty setter and eat burgers till his stomach ached!

"Where did you get that collar?" he demanded.

Carface puffed his cigar. Clouds of smoke swirled around his beady eyes. "Buddy of mine has 'em."

"Can I meet him?" Charlie was eager.

But Itchy was in his way. "Charlie, you can't trust Carface. He shouldn't have gotten into heaven in the first place."

Carface blew smoke in Itchy's snout. The small dog coughed and wheezed.

Charlie said under his breath, "Relax, Itch. I can handle this guy."

"What about the horn?" Itchy coughed.

Charlie ignored him. "Lead on, Carface," he said.

Itchy struggled to keep up with the bigger dogs. "Wait up! Wiener dog, here. Short legs!"

Itchy caught up with Charlie and Carface on Eldridge Street, in a rough part of town. A strange old shop crouched in the middle of the block. Charlie read the sign:

RED'S CURIOS
Psychic Readings
and Trophies

"Hey, Itch, we can get our palms read and bronzed at the same time," Charlie joked as Carface stepped inside the cluttered store.

The bulldog cried, "Red, customers!"

Charlie didn't see any trophies inside. The place was filled with dusty knickknacks and mummified bats, antique toys, and strange things whose purpose Charlie couldn't even guess at. A cat-shaped clock swung its tail and tick-tocked loudly on the wall.

Itchy's eyes started to water. His nose felt all stuffed up. He searched the strange shop for a cat. Cats made Itchy itch. But Itchy didn't see any cats.

A pair of shabby curtains parted. With a nasty hacking cough, a feeble old dog shuffled out of the back room. "Hello," he wheezed.

Carface began, "Red, meet a couple of friends of mine—"

"—Charlie Barkin, Itchy Itchiford, welcome," Red finished the bulldog's sentence.

Charlie said, "Wait, how could he—?"

"See you?" Carface asked. "Red's into all kinds of mumbo jumbo. You'll love him." Carface turned to the old dog. "These boys have come to do a little shopping."

Itchy's nose twitched. "You got cats around here or what?"

"Cats? Good heavens, no!" Red chuckled.

Itchy stifled a sneeze. He couldn't understand it. He usually only sneezed around cats.

"Carface tells us you've got some special collars," Charlie said, warming up to con a fresh victim. He was sure he could trick the old dog out of those collars.

"Collars, yes," said Red. "They're going to be the next big thing. Here, enjoy." The old dog casually tossed a collar to the eager shepherd.

"What's the catch, old man?" the dachshund asked.

"No catch. Any friend of Carface is a friend of mine," Red said innocently. Then he added, "Oh, there is one small thing."

"I knew it. We're out of here." Itchy headed for the door, but he stopped when he saw that Charlie hadn't followed him.

Red mumbled and wheezed a bit, then he said, "The collars are only good until sundown tomorrow. After that you'll be, shall we say, *insubstantial* again."

"By then I'll have Sasha begging for me," Charlie said, and he put on the collar. "A perfect fit." Charlie tingled and sparkled, and . . . he was solid again!

"It feels great to be back in the flesh!" Charlie cried. He scooped a deck of cards off a table. His nimble paws flipped and fanned the cardboard squares.

Carface stuck another collar over Itchy's head. But the dachshund was not as happy. The second his collar turned him solid, he burst into a gigantic sneeze and discovered he was swarming with fleas. "I'm infested again!" he said.

Carface hurried them out of the shop. "Have fun, boys!"

Charlie looked over his shoulder. "I owe you one, Red."

Carface closed the door. Then Red cackled and said, "You'll owe me one all right!"

The bulldog laughed. "They fell for it. When we get that horn, we can open any safe or bank vault in the world!" Carface howled with glee.

"Silence!" Red hissed. "I didn't recruit you for such entry-level wickedness. You have so much to learn about being bad. You've been vicious. You've cheated and lied, schemed and swindled, but you're still an amateur."

"I answered your ad, didn't I?" Carface

protested. He waved a piece of paper. "Money! Power! Stature! Call 1-800-BRIMSTONE for free info."

Red chuckled. "Oh, you're working with a master now. I'll teach you wicked ways you've never known before." As the old dog spoke, he underwent a terrible transformation. Horns poked from his forehead. His tail grew longer. "Charlie doesn't know it, but he's in my power. And by sunset I'll have Gabriel's horn!"

By the time Red finished speaking, he was a monstrous, glowing-red demon cat.

"Why can't I get the horn?" Carface demanded.

Red's paw sprouted five daggerlike claws. He shredded a sofa. "I trusted you, and you bungled your chance," the demon cat roared.

"I could try again, boss," Carface offered.

"You'll never find it. Only angels can hear its heavenly tone," Red said.

"But I'm an angel," Carface replied.

Red's grin revealed razor-sharp fangs. "Not anymore. You work for me now, remember? Soon you'll know the pleasure of being the lowest of the low. It feels so good to be bad!"

Chapter 3

"Not bad singing for a stray," the master of ceremonies said. From behind his desk, the big Labrador looked Sasha up and down. Both of them ignored the country-western singer by the door.

"Thanks, can I have my prize now?" Sasha asked.

The Lab opened a drawer and pulled out a large soup bone with a cheap blue ribbon tied around it.

"You advertised a *meal* for the winner," Sasha complained.

The Labrador leaned across his desk. "I get off work at ten. We can have dinner . . . together."

"I'd rather go hungry," Sasha said. Then she slapped the soup bone into the country singer's paws. Sasha slammed the door as she left.

Sasha was hungry, and she had another mouth to feed. So she slipped into the buffet line.

Sasha was quietly filling a sack with food when Charlie sauntered up to her. "You must hear this all the time," Charlie began, "but you sing like an angel." He winked at Itchy.

The little dachshund looked worried. He'd already reminded Charlie about the horn a dozen times. But Charlie whispered, "Relax. Take notes, Itchy. You're about to watch a master."

Charlie knew he could charm the fleas off anybody. Sasha was bound to come around. "The name's Barkin, Charlie Barkin. And you are . . . ?"

"Not even remotely interested," Sasha said frostily.

"Let me help you with the bag," Charlie offered.

But Sasha wouldn't let go. "Please, I don't want a scene," she whispered.

"Still looking for free eats?" The Labrador walked across the room. "You've got to pay for that, sister."

Charlie saw his chance. "I'll take care of this," he said gallantly. He turned to the Lab. "Put it on Carface's tab."

The Labrador grunted and went back to his office.

"Now, where were we?" Charlie asked, as he turned to Sasha. But the setter was gone! Only her bag of food remained.

Itchy waddled up to his friend. "I noted how you swept the lady off her paws."

Charlie shrugged. "So I'm rusty." He raised his eyebrows. "Let's make a little home delivery."

Charlie grabbed Sasha's bag and dashed down the street.

"I'm never going to get back to heaven," Itchy sighed. He raced to catch up with Charlie. "Short legs, Charlie. Short legs!" They panted up and down the steep hills of San Francisco. "Something tells me you're forgetting about the horn," the little dachshund gasped.

"The what?" Charlie mumbled through the mouthful of bag he was carrying.

The running dogs glimpsed Sasha's coppery coat at the top of Mathers Street. The setter ducked into the overgrown yard of an abandoned brownstone building. Charlie and Itchy followed her.

Sasha had a cozy home in the brownstone's deserted garden.

Poking his head through a break in an old wooden fence, Charlie caught his breath, smiled his best smile, and said, "Nice digs."

Sasha whipped around and bared her teeth. "You again. What do you want?" she growled.

Charlie put the bag on the ground. "You left your doggie bag."

Sasha's face softened. "Oh, thanks."

"There's enough food for two," Charlie said hopefully. "If you want some company—"

"Sorry, I have a kid," Sasha replied quickly.

"I'm good with kids," Charlie persisted.

Then they heard a big yawn. A sleepy eight-year-old human emerged from an old toolshed. The boy saw the bag and pounced on it. He greedily shoveled food into his mouth. "Thanks, girl, I was starving!" he said in human language.

The boy stopped eating long enough to hug Sasha. Then he went right back to stuffing himself.

"Oh, she's got a *kid* kid," Charlie said to Itchy.

Turning to Sasha, Charlie asked, "What did he do—follow you home?"

The little boy stopped eating. His eyes bugged out. He gasped in amazement. "You can *talk*!"

"Don't encourage him," Itchy said.

The boy screeched. Sasha ran to his side, barking at Charlie. She was speaking *Caninese*, like all dogs, so Charlie knew she was saying, "He can *understand* you?"

"Well, of course he can understand us."

"Holy cow!" the boy exclaimed.

"Holy dogs, actually," Charlie began. "I'm Charlie and this is Itchy."

"I'm David," the boy said slowly.

Sasha just growled. She was as frightened as David. Dogs simply didn't speak like humans. This was unnatural! Sasha grabbed the boy's pant leg and tried to pull him away from Charlie and Itchy.

"Don't be scared," Charlie said.

Sasha and David broke into a run. Charlie sprinted to cut them off. "I'm a good dog, really!" he said. "The truth is, I'm an angel."

David stopped and looked around suspiciously. "Come on. Somebody's playing a trick." He imagined that someone was hiding and using a microphone or throwing their voice.

Charlie was annoyed that this kid didn't believe him. "Okay. If I'm not an angel, how can I do this?"

Charlie thought back to his basic flying lessons, took a little run, and leaped. He landed in a pile of trash. The kid laughed. Charlie pulled himself out of the heap. "Run, jump, fly, what did I forget?" he wondered. Charlie adjusted his collar absently. "Something's wrong, Itchy." Then suddenly Charlie knew what the problem was. "The collars!"

The German shepherd turned to David. "Kid, this will make a believer of you." He winked at Sasha, cracked his knuckles, and pulled off his collar.

Charlie magically disappeared! Setter and boy were shocked. Then a soft voice said, "Woof!" behind the puzzled pair.

For a few minutes, Charlie vanished and reappeared in a variety of places. He was on the fence, on the edge of a roof, and then he was standing in front of them saying, "Tah-dah!"

David said, "That was great! I can do magic too." He took a small red ball from his pocket and made it disappear. Then he took the ball from Itchy's ear. "Tah-dah!"

"Wow! What else can you do?" Itchy asked.

Charlie turned up his charm and said to Sasha, "Kid's good. I could help him with his technique."

Sasha frowned and backed Charlie away from David. "He needs help getting home. He's lost."

They glanced over at the boy, who was entertaining Itchy with more magic tricks.

"I don't know how you talk to him, but please ask him where he lives," Sasha begged.

"Why don't *you* ask him," Charlie said.

Sasha sighed. "That would be a miracle."

"One miracle coming up!" Charlie laughed. He whipped off his collar. Charlie was instantly invisible, and Sasha felt a warm muzzle kiss hers. Sparks tingled all around her mouth. She barked, and it sounded like human speech!

"Of all the stuck-up mutts I've met, you're the worst!" Sasha sputtered as Charlie reappeared. He settled the collar back around his neck.

David dropped his magic wand and stared at Sasha. "Now *you* talk!" Then he shifted his gaze to Charlie. "You must be my guardian angel. My mom told me everyone has a guardian angel. You're here because I ran away from home, right?"

"Uh, right, kid." Charlie hugged the boy and Sasha. "We'll make some team, huh?"

Sasha was upset with David. "Hold it. You mean you're not lost?"

"Not anymore. I've got my guardian angel," the boy said with a smile.

"But why did you run away?" Sasha asked.

David turned to Charlie. He was sure his guardian angel knew all about him, even the sad part about Mom dying. "Go ahead, you tell her."

Itchy muttered, "This ought to be good."

"It's—it's school," Charlie stammered, searching for the right answer. "Bullies? No. You're having, um, kid problems?"

David nodded. "With my stepmom."

Charlie smiled smugly. "I knew it!"

"She wants me to call her Mom," said David. "But she's not my *real* mom. I'm never going home again."

"What are you going to do, live on the street?" Sasha demanded.

David nodded. "Yup, and do my magic at Cannery Square. Tourists give you money."

"That's silly," Sasha scolded. "Tell me where you live."

David was defiant. "No!"

Sasha knew she was losing the fight. She

turned to Charlie for help. "Will you set him straight?"

"Sounds like a good plan to me, David," Charlie said agreeably.

Sasha fumed. "You call yourself a guardian angel?"

"He's not ready to go home," Charlie explained.

"He's only eight years old," Sasha argued.

"That's 56 in dog years," Charlie countered.

David smiled. He liked this dog.

Charlie put a paw across David's shoulders. He had a plan. He would teach David a thing or two, stay around Sasha, and *eventually* help David realize that he belonged at home.

David gathered his magic gear. He left the yard with Charlie. Sasha followed to keep an eye on them, which suited Charlie just fine!

The dogs and David strolled on Inglewood Street. They passed a small green park across the street from a police station. Charlie fell into pace with Sasha. "So is there a Mister Sasha?" he asked.

"No, and I'm not taking applications," Sasha said.

"Okay, okay. But if you were, what qualities would you be looking for?" asked Charlie.

"Oh, I don't know," Sasha said. "Loyalty, strength, humility, compassion . . ."

Charlie was listening intently to Sasha and not paying attention to where he was going. He suddenly crashed into a telephone pole. *"Ooof!"* he said.

" . . . and of course, style," said Sasha.

"You hear that?" Itchy's ears jerked straight up.

Charlie heard it, too—the beautiful note of Gabriel's horn. Both dog angels looked around wildly. They saw an ice-cream vendor and a woman pushing a baby carriage. Police officers went in and out the doors of the busy police station.

"Itch! It's got to be the horn!" Charlie cried.

Itchy slapped a paw over Charlie's mouth. *"Shh!"*

"There it is!" Itchy exclaimed. His nose pointed at a policeman. The officer's head was wrapped in a bandage. He carried the horn into the police station. Gabriel's horn was dull and dented, but the dogs recognized it by its heavenly hum.

"Go get it, Itch! I'll stay here with Sasha," Charlie commanded.

Itchy refused. "That's *your* job."

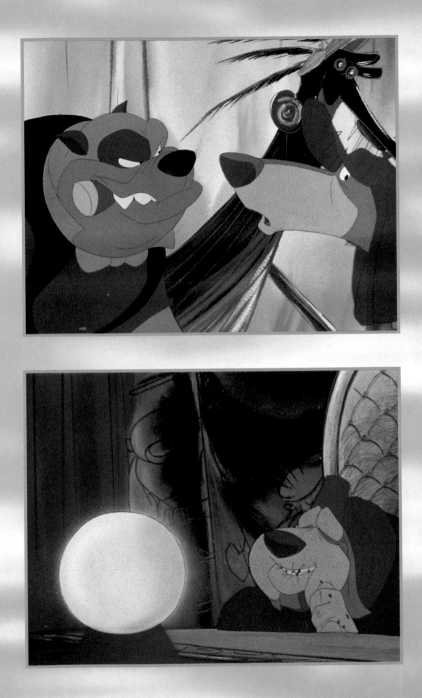

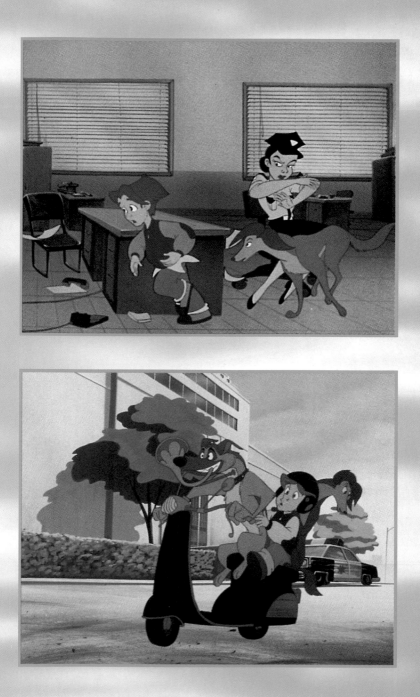

"Okay," Charlie sighed. "I'll be back before you can say hallelujah." Charlie trotted across the street.

"Where is he going?" David asked as the dogs settled on the cool green grass.

"Eh, confidential guardian angel business," Itchy said. He watched Charlie sit in front of the glass doors of the police station. The shepherd panted and wagged his tail. A pair of officers came out of the glass doors. One patted Charlie on the head. Just before the glass doors closed, Charlie bolted between them.

Charlie had no trouble at all getting into the police station. The pair of cops at the reception desk were busy. Around them, people waited on benches. A janitor mopped the floor. No one paid any attention to the dog.

"Where's the Lost-and-Found?" Charlie asked.

The desk officer didn't even look up from his newspaper. "Room 112, through the squad room."

"Ten-four," Charlie said in cop lingo for "that's all."

Charlie kept in the shadows. He slipped from wastebasket to copy machine to file cabinet, staying low and thinking invisible thoughts. He sneaked past a desk where a young man and woman talked to a worried officer.

"Mr. and Mrs. Hart, I'm Officer Reyes. We spoke last night on the phone." She took a photo from Mrs. Hart's shaking hand. "This will help," Officer Reyes said. "Now why do you think he ran away?"

"It could only be one thing," Thom Hart stated.

His wife, Claire, said, "We're having a baby, and David got very upset when I told him."

If Charlie had listened to the conversation, he would have learned that David's parents were worried sick about him. But all Charlie could think about was getting back Gabriel's horn. He missed his chance to reunite David with his parents.

Charlie followed the horn's steady hum to Room 112. Officer Logan Winsett placed a tag on the tarnished, dented horn. He couldn't hear the heavenly humming. To him it was just another piece of lost-and-found.

Logan put the horn on one of the many shelves inside the chain-link fence that made Room 112. He used to play trumpet in his high-school band, so Logan looked around the empty room and gave the horn a little toot.

Instantly, because of the horn's magic, the chain-link cage opened and everything inside with a lid or in a box popped open! Officer Winsett found himself in a shower of lost-and-found. He hurried to get everything back on its shelf.

Charlie jumped at the chain-link gate just as it swung shut. *What can I do now?* he wondered.

Then the shepherd remembered his demonstration in the alley. So he took off the collar. The wire grid tickled as Charlie drifted through the fence.

Charlie found the horn right away. He carried it past Logan, easy as pie. Then Charlie glided through the fence, but the horn didn't!

Ka-bong! The trumpet fell to the concrete floor.

Logan was startled. He wondered how the strange horn got from its shelf to the gate. Logan scratched his head and put the horn back where it belonged.

Charlie looked at the troublesome instrument. Then he glanced at the small opening in the chain-link fence. He griped, "Of course, it couldn't be Gabriel's flute or Gabriel's kazoo. *Nooooo.* That would be too easy."

Chapter 4

Sasha was one confused Irish setter. This was all too crazy. Her boy wasn't really a stray. He'd run away from home! And now Charlie and Itchy, who were dogs—but really angels—were trying to get something out of a police station. Itchy insisted their mission was a secret. Charlie had gone into the station and then a few minutes later popped up out of nowhere.

"Miss me?" he asked.

Itchy wanted to know where the you-know-what was. And that's when Charlie said, "Minor setback. We'll have to raid the place."

"*Raid the place?*" Sasha cried. Sasha couldn't understand why they would do that.

So Charlie quickly told everyone the secret of the horn. Charlie had a plan to recover the instrument, and it sounded like his idea would work. Sasha, Itchy, and David followed him back to the station house.

Once at the station house, David put on a pair of dark glasses and took hold of three leashes attached to Charlie, Itchy, and Sasha.

Trying to look as innocent as possible, David and the three dogs waltzed into the police station. David was pretending to be a blind boy with three Seeing Eye dogs.

The trick would have worked if a mean-looking police dog hadn't spotted Itchy and caused a police officer to spill his coffee during the commotion. "Who let those dogs in here?" shouted the officer.

Sensing trouble, Charlie called out to the others, "Plan B, guys!"

David shouted, "Donuts! Fresh off the truck!"

In the confusion that followed David's announcement, Sasha and Itchy raced through the police station creating a huge distraction.

Coffee cups bounced off desks. Chairs toppled. Lamps fell to the floor. Papers flew like snow in a blizzard. In all the confusion, no one noticed Charlie strolling calmly into the station.

As police officers tried to catch the other dogs, Sasha grabbed Officer Logan Winsett's keys and tossed them to Itchy. Itchy tossed the keys to David.

As the boy ran toward the Lost-and-Found cage, where Charlie waited, he ran right into a policeman and knocked him down. David stopped to help the man to his feet. Then someone yelled, "Stop that kid!"

David saw Officer Winsett coming across the squad room. "Okay, son. Give me the keys," he said. Logan stopped beside the other cop. Both police officers held out their hands.

"Nothing up my sleeve, sir," David said. His hands were behind his back. Then he magically produced a pair of handcuffs and snapped them around the policemen's wrists.

"What's that behind your ear?" David asked playfully. He reached behind Logan's ear and jangled the keys. "You've been a great audience."

David got the keys to Charlie. The shepherd opened the chain-link gate. In an instant, he returned with Gabriel's horn in his paws.

Charlie and his friends ran through the jumbled squad room. David was so worried about being chased that he didn't look in front of him. He ran *smack* into Officer Reyes. For a moment they were face-to-face.

The policewoman couldn't believe her eyes. Here was the very boy she was looking for! But then he was gone!

When he got across the street, Charlie placed the horn gently on the grass.

"Sasha, great moves," he told the setter. "Itch, just like old times," he added to his friend. Charlie tousled David's hair. "And you'd make a great dog."

"Freeze! Sit! Stay!" Officer Reyes shouted as she ran through the station's front doors and across to the park.

"It's the dog pound for sure!" Itchy screeched.

Charlie hopped on an unattended motor scooter. "Let's go!"

Hopping on, David shouted, "Let's haul!" Sasha jumped aboard too.

Itchy was too slow. He could only watch as Charlie zoomed off. "Wait!" cried Itchy. "Short legs! Short legs!"

Itchy thought he could fly to the motor scooter. He launched himself into the air, but he accidentally landed on top of a police car!

Officer Reyes was driving the cruiser. She was determined to get that boy!

Itchy clutched the bubble lights as the police car screeched around the corner. The little dog howled, *"Whoooaaaahh!"*

David zigzagged through an intersection with his eyes squeezed shut. Horns blared. Cars zipped by, swerving to avoid the speeding scooter.

Sasha screamed, "Aren't guardian angels supposed to protect people?"

Charlie answered, "Hey, it's my first day on the job."

The patrol car was close behind. As Officer Reyes crossed the street, she flicked on the siren. The siren's speaker was right next to Itchy's head! His ears shook with the shrill wail.

Picnickers in Nob Hill Park were very surprised to see a motor scooter driven by a German shepherd, chased by a police car, riding over the grass. Car and motorcycle crisscrossed all the way down Lombard Street.

When the two vehicles passed close to each other, Itchy screamed, "I'm gonna barf!"

Charlie had no time to answer. He tried holding the motor scooter steady but nearly tipped over. His ears flapped in the wind. Charlie was having the time of his life. This kind of stuff never happened in heaven!

The police car chased the motor scooter through stalls heaped with fish. They demolished dozens of booths. The catch-of-the-day rained down on Fisherman's Wharf.

Officer Reyes slammed on her brakes and skidded to a stop just shy of a garbage truck blocking the street. She switched off her siren. There was no point in continuing the chase now.

Itchy jumped off the cruiser and onto the speeding motor scooter.

Charlie looked around at the sparkling bay and Golden Gate Bridge gleaming in the sunshine. Even the ugly ruined prison on Alcatraz Island looked beautiful!

"Sure beats harp lessons, hey, Itch?" Charlie laughed. Itchy shook his head. The siren was still ringing in his ears.

Sasha said, "Let's get David out of here!"

Chapter 5

"You're going to love this place, boss. It's got everything you wanted." Carface was sure he'd done a good job this time. He was eager to prove himself after losing Gabriel's horn. Red wanted a headquarters, and Carface had found him the perfect spot: Alcatraz Prison.

"Beachfront location, fenced yard, tight security." Carface continued the tour.

Red regarded level upon level of empty dirty cells. Water dripped through filthy cracks. Rusty cell doors creaked on their massive hinges. "All that, and ratatouille too," the demon cat snarled. He snatched a rat from a rusty railing. *Crunch, crunch, crunch.*

Carface shuddered and returned to his tour speech. "The joint's been home to some great pedigrees: Capone, 'Machine Gun' Kelly, the Bird Dog of Alcatraz . . ."

"Very impressive." Red swallowed the rat.

"Then I did good?" Carface asked eagerly.

"Indeed, have a bone." Red picked a rat bone from his fangs. He stuck the bone in Carface's mouth. With a puff of flame from his claw tip, Red lit the bone cigar.

"You dogs have enjoyed things for far too long. Wouldn't you agree, Carface?" Red purred.

"Yeah, whatever you say, Boss." Carface was just happy to please the hotshot.

"Fortunately, all that will come to a spectacular end tonight," Red said. He stretched and added, "I feel like purring. It's just so good to be bad!"

Red spread his paws. Dark clouds churned in the sky.

"What do you mean we're not going back yet? We got the horn," Itchy said.

The little dachshund stood beside a pile of nets, crab traps, floats, and other fishing gear on the crowded wharf.

Charlie put down the horn and said, "I still need to take care of David. I *am* his guardian angel."

Itchy saw the pretty setter waiting nearby with the boy. "Yeah, and Sasha has nothing to do with it."

Charlie sighed. Itchy knew him too well. "Well . . ."

Itchy's skin crawled with fleas. And the thought of failing in his heavenly mission made him even more itchy. "You're making me crazy!"

"Just a little more time," Charlie said, as he put Gabriel's horn in one of the crab traps. "The horn will be safe here." Then he gently kicked the trap over the side of the dock. *Kersplash!* Horn and trap disappeared beneath the briny bay.

Charlie and Itchy trotted up the wharf to join Sasha and David. Fisherman's Wharf bustled with tourists in busy shops and cafés. Charlie could smell all kinds of good things to eat: sourdough bread, fried crab cakes, and, of course, double-chili cheeseburgers. Charlie led his friends through the crowded streets full of all the noise and grit he'd missed so much in heaven.

For a moment the German shepherd thought he was lost. Then he suddenly glimpsed a street sign:

> CANNERY SQUARE

Dogs and boy rushed to join the crush of magicians, musicians, and mimes entertaining the excited crowd.

"This is your big chance. Are you nervous?" Charlie asked.

David rubbed damp palms on his pants. "A little—and sweaty."

"Well, don't be," Charlie said.

"Excited?" Itchy prompted.

David grinned. "You bet!"

Sasha was worried. The boy was still just a puppy. Performing on the street could be tough. "Now Charlie . . ." she fretted.

Charlie winked at the setter. "It's okay."

David put his cap on the sidewalk. Then he burst into song. And while he sang, he performed magic tricks. A small family watched him for a while, but they didn't leave a coin. Many other people walked past David, drawn away by one of the other performers. Some just smiled.

Then the dark clouds that had been forming over Alcatraz rolled over the square. Tourists and performers scrambled for cover as heavy raindrops pelted the pavement.

Cannery Square emptied like a magician's trick milk pitcher. In seconds, the crowds had disappeared.

Charlie said, "C'mon. Let's get out of the rain."

The friends huddled miserably under an awning. David sneezed. Despite their fur, all the dogs were soon shivering. There were only a few small coins in David's soggy money cap. David was discouraged.

Itchy tried to lighten the moment. "I'm so hungry I could eat a Reebok." He turned to the downcast boy. "How about you?"

David tried to smile, but his lips sagged.

"I thought so," Itchy said. "I'll be right back."

Itchy trotted to a Chinese restaurant across the street. David looked into the front window. A little girl sat between her parents. She slurped steaming noodles from a big bowl.

David's mouth watered. A hot tear joined the cool rain on his cheeks. He turned to the shepherd, "Charlie, can my mom see me from heaven?"

Charlie nodded. "Of course she can, kiddo."

Charlie and Sasha snuggled closer to the little boy.

"But you still have your dad and stepmom here, don't forget," Sasha said gently.

"My stepmom doesn't want me," David said sadly. "She's having her own kid."

Charlie glanced at Sasha. Now they understood! The pup had left home because his stepmom was going to have a baby of her own. He was afraid she didn't want him.

"Parents can love more than one pup," Sasha said. "Maybe she just didn't know how to tell you that."

"You should give her another chance," Charlie advised in his best guardian-angel voice.

David shook his head, no.

Charlie knew how the boy felt. "I ran away from home when *I* was little," Charlie said.

"I'll bet that upset your parents," said Sasha.

"I don't know," said Charlie. "I never saw them after that. Guess I could have used a guardian angel, huh?"

"I'll go home with you, Charlie," said David. "If you promise to take me."

"I promise," said Charlie.

David nodded and hugged Charlie. Sasha smiled tenderly.

"You've got to try this moo goo gai pan!" Itchy yelped. The chubby dachshund waddled up, lugging a heavy Chinese takeout box.

While David and Itchy enjoyed the delicious food, Sasha murmured, "Nice work, Charlie Barkin. You really are an angel."

"Right now, I'd give anything not to be," Charlie choked. He felt strange and sort of tingly. "I have to go back soon."

"Oh, right. Of course," said Sasha. "So, is there a Mrs. Charlie in heaven?"

"Oh no, nothing like that," Charlie said sincerely.

"No?" said Sasha. "Why not?"

The tingling was stronger. Charlie sighed. "Because I never met anyone like you. Not even in heaven."

Sasha could see the love in the shepherd's deep brown eyes. "Oh, Charlie, I'll always be with you," Sasha promised. They were part of each other now.

"Charlie, you're disappearing!" Sasha cried.

Now he knew what the tingling was. Charlie looked at his transparent paw. "Not now!" Was it sunset already?

Itchy's collar also sputtered and vanished. The dachshund faded from sight as thunder rolled through the sky.

David looked around. "Charlie, Itchy! Come out, you guys. No more tricks."

"They're gone," Sasha said.

"Charlie wouldn't leave. He's my guardian angel." David was right. Charlie was standing in front of the boy waving his invisible paws and shouting, "I'm here! Right here!"

Charlie knew exactly what to do. The big shepherd and the little dachshund raced along rain-slicked streets. The lights of the city glittered in puddles.

Itchy still thought they should take the horn back to heaven. But somehow Charlie couldn't let David down. Charlie just couldn't help himself. Deep down he was a good dog—and always a sucker for a cute pup.

Charlie doubled his speed. He left his friend behind. "Short legs!" Itchy cried. But Charlie couldn't wait.

An invisible Charlie rushed through the locked door of Red's Curios. Charlie barked, "Red, you've got to help me!"

Red and Carface looked up from their card

game. The cat clock tick-tocked softly. Red rose to his feet. "Anything, Charlie. Just name it."

"I need a new collar," Charlie panted.

Red's face wrinkled with glee. "You enjoyed it. I knew you would."

"So, how about it?" Charlie asked.

"If you want another collar, you must pay," Red said. The cat clock ticked louder.

"I don't have any cash," Charlie said. "How about an I.O.U.?"

No one could have looked sadder than Red. "I'm sorry. Carface will show you out." The old dog eased back into his seat and picked up his cards.

"There must be some way to make a deal," said Charlie.

Carface whispered, "He might take a trade."

Charlie stopped and thought a moment. "Oh, Red. I have this . . . horn."

"Sorry, I'm not musical."

Desperate, Charlie warmed up his pitch. "It's more than a horn. There's nothing like it in all the world."

"Let me sleep on it," Red said wearily.

But Charlie was even more desperate. "I don't have that kind of time."

There was a bright little gleam in Red's eye,

and he smiled. "I like your spirit, Charlie. Bring me this horn, and you can have your collar."

Charlie turned to leave, then he said, "Um, I need the collar to get the horn. You can trust me."

"This isn't about trust, Charlie. We have a deal," the old dog stated. The clock stopped ticking, and Red held out his paw.

"Charlie!" Itchy flew through the closed door. But the little dog was too late.

Charlie and Red were shaking hands. And the shepherd said, "Deal."

A wisp of smoke rose from their joined paws. Charlie glowed. Then something coiled around Charlie's neck. The coil slithered and wriggled and became a collar.

Then old dog Red's ears grew taller and his muzzle got shorter. Before Itchy and Charlie's astonished eyes, Red became his true self—a demon cat!

"Guess the cat's out of the bag, eh?" Red teased. "Now be a good little bow-wow and fetch me my horn!"

"What have you done?!" Itchy cried.

Charlie didn't know what to do. Up till then, he'd always been the con artist. Now *he'd* been conned! Charlie didn't have time to think much more. The demon cat spat a fireball!

Charlie ran for the exit. The door opened for him, then slammed shut. A ghostlike Itchy zipped through the glass, hot on the heels of his friend.

Sasha was trying to take David home. But neither one could figure out how to read the map in the Bay Area Rapid Transit station.

"Which train goes to North Bay?" Sasha wondered.

David looked at the maze of twisted colored lines. "I can't tell. If Charlie were here, he'd know."

Sasha put her paw on David's shoulder to comfort him. Then they heard Charlie call their names. The friendly shepherd was with them again! "I had to come back. I wouldn't be a guardian angel if I didn't."

Sasha was about to give Charlie a welcome-back kiss, when Itchy squealed, "Are you nuts? You gave away the horn!"

"It was a bluff," Charlie explained. The clever shepherd had a new plan all worked out. "David's going back home. The horn's going back to heaven."

"Who are you talking to?" Sasha asked.

Itchy was still invisible to everyone but Charlie.

"You shook on it! You made a deal with him." Itchy was horrified. How could Charlie be working with the other side?

"*You* didn't make a deal with him. That's why you're taking the horn back," Charlie explained.

Itchy was skeptical. "Me?"

But the argument was over as soon as Carface appeared out of the shadows. "I knew you couldn't be trusted," the bulldog snarled. He grabbed David.

Charlie leaped to defend the boy, but his magic collar tightened around his neck. He gasped for breath.

Carface hauled David to the roof of a waiting commuter train. As the train pulled out of the station, Carface called back to Charlie, "Bring the item to Alcatraz in one hour, or junior here doesn't have a prayer." With that, the train disappeared down the tracks.

Chapter 6

"Where is he? The hour is up," Red demanded. His voice drowned out the crashing waves and howling wind outside Alcatraz. David shivered on an iron bed frame in a damp prison cell.

Carface tried to calm the hotshot. "You know what they say, boss, patience is a—"

Red stomped his hoof. A flaming crack opened in the concrete floor.

Carface gulped. "Maybe he's stuck in traffic," he suggested lamely.

"What kind of dog are you? You sold out to a mangy old cat!" David challenged.

Red's big yellow eyes glared at the boy.

"Quiet! Or I'll have your tongue!" he roared.

Suddenly Charlie's cheerful voice echoed off the dank prison walls. "Red! The horn." He held Gabriel's horn so Red and Carface could see it, then they let the shepherd step into David's cell.

"Let *me,* boss," Carface said. "*I'll* fetch it for you." Carface fumbled with the horn, and it skidded across the stained concrete. It rolled to a stop at Red's feet.

Red snatched up the magical horn. "It's mine! *Mine!*"

Charlie and David ran for the cell door even as the gates shut. They made it through in the nick of time.

Carface wanted to chase them. But Red refused. He had what he wanted. Red put the horn to his lips and began to play. The music was chilling, eerie, ominous.

Red's dark tune soon reached the clouds. The sky was stirred like a boiling pot of witch's brew. Whitecaps whipped the bay into a churning froth.

Charlie and his friends were on the Alcatraz wharf climbing into a boat when the stars began to fall. Charlie blinked through the pouring rain. Were those stars? No! They were dog angels dropping from heaven. Red was capturing them!

But there was even worse news. The more Red played, the bigger and bigger he grew. Soon he was a towering giant.

Charlie groaned. What had he done? He had bungled scams before, but this was a disaster!

"Come on, jump!" Sasha cried to Charlie from the boat as it rocked on the tossing waves. David and Itchy huddled beside the setter.

"No, this is all my fault!" said Charlie. He pushed the boat away from the wharf. "Get David home safely!"

The last cell clanged shut on the last dog angel. All the angels were now imprisoned.

"Welcome, boys!" Red laughed. Then he clapped his hands. The island shuddered, and a wall of steam rose around it. Alcatraz began to sink into the bay like an elevator in a liquid shaft.

"You're in for a hot time tonight!" Red gloated. "It's a cat's world now."

Not as long as Charlie Barkin had breath in his body! The brave shepherd raced back inside Alcatraz and lunged at Red. In an instant they were rolling on the floor, fighting like, well, cats and dogs.

First Red had the horn, then Charlie. At a wave of Red's paw, Charlie's collar tightened. He dropped the horn. The demon cat seized the trumpet and raised it to smash Charlie's skull.

But something stopped him. Someone had handcuffed Red's tail to a cell door. It was David! He, Itchy, and Sasha had returned to the prison to help Charlie!

Charlie and his friends fought the giant cat. With the four of them working together, they managed to make Red lose track of the horn.

Suddenly the cat spotted Charlie escaping with the horn in his mouth. Now Red was furious. Charlie dashed up a long flight of stairs onto the roof of Alacatraz. Red burst through the roof after him.

Still clutching the horn, Charlie scrambled up a water tower.

The giant cat paused. Would it be safe to climb the tower? Seeing Charlie with the horn blinded Red to the danger. He began scaling the tower. But when Red reached the top, the tower bent, then snapped! Red plummeted through the roof into the dark swirling water of the bay.

David, Itchy, and Sasha were in shock. What had happened to Charlie?

Suddenly someone laughed. It was the shepherd! He had survived the collapse of the tower—and he still had Gabriel's horn!

Charlie smiled, put the horn to his lips, and blew for all he was worth.

Instantly the horn gleamed like new again, and Charlie played a song as heavenly as any ever heard. Alcatraz Island began to rise above the waves. Every cell door swung open. And all the angel dogs floated up to heaven, singing Charlie's tune. The sea grew calm. The dark clouds blew away.

The demon screamed as the golden horn took away his evil powers. The cat quickly shrank back to his normal size and was sucked down into one of the prison's crevices.

Charlie bounded over to Sasha, Itchy, and David. "Everyone okay?" the shepherd asked.

"Where's Red?" Carface asked mournfully.

"His boss yanked his leash," Charlie replied.

"Good riddance," Carface said. He spat on the ground. "Charlie, I hope you didn't take any of this personally. I was just playing the game."

"Sure, Carface," Charlie agreed. "Say, what did you trade Red for your collar?"

"He wanted the bottom of my shoes or somethin'. Ha, ha. I don't even wear shoes, stupid cat." Carface cackled.

Then the ground split open.

"Stupid dog! It was your *soul*!" Red's voice thundered. His arm slithered out of the crack to grip the bulldog's ankle. Carface squealed as he slid through the hole. The crack closed again.

"I thought all dogs went to heaven," Itchy said.

Chapter 7

"C'mon, Charlie. Anabelle's calling us," Itchy barked.

A golden shaft of light came down from the clouds.

"Thanks for letting me be your guardian angel," Charlie said to David. He tousled the boy's hair. "Sasha can take you home now."

David tried to smile, but he had to hold back his tears. "Charlie, don't go," the boy sniffled.

"I'll always be with you," Charlie said. He picked up Gabriel's horn.

Charlie and Itchy stepped toward the shaft of light. The shepherd removed the magic collar. It vaporized before it hit the ground.

As the angel dogs rose inside the golden column of light, Charlie said, "Sasha, I love . . ."

"And I love you," Sasha said.

On their way up to heaven, the angel dogs suddenly stopped in midair.

"What's wrong? Is this thing stuck between floors?" Itchy wondered.

Then Anabelle was beside them. "I'll take the horn from here, Charles," the whippet said. She reached for the golden trumpet. Charlie handed it over.

"What? You're afraid I'll drop it?" Charlie asked.

"No, there's someone who still needs to go back where he belongs," Anabelle said.

Charlie was confused. "David?"

"You, Charlie. For what you've done, you deserve something special." Anabelle smiled. She held up a shining first-class angel wings pin. "Claim these in, say, 20 years," Anabelle added sweetly.

It took a moment for Charlie to understand what the whippet meant. Then he was overjoyed! "Itchy, you hear that? We're going back!"

Itchy shook his head. "Not this dog. When you can fly, short legs don't matter."

Charlie hugged the dachshund. "Take care of yourself, buddy."

Then Anabelle and Itchy rose into the golden light. Charlie found himself hanging in midair. He knew what to do next.

David led Sasha up the sidewalk toward a cozy cottage overlooking San Francisco Bay. A big cloud of dust exploded in front of them. As the dust settled, Charlie became visible.

"Can you believe it? I got a weekend pass for the rest of my life!" Charlie exclaimed as David and Sasha hugged him.

"Thom, it's David!" Mrs. Hart cried.

David's stepmother ran to the boy. She hugged him and cried, "We were so worried about you!"

"You worried about me?" David asked.

Mrs. Hart answered, "Of course. Having this baby doesn't mean I don't love you. Honey, we're a family."

"And pretty soon a bigger one," David's dad added.

David glanced at the dogs. "Uh, Dad, I'm glad you brought up that bigger family stuff."

While the Harts discussed the matter of pets and leashes and who was going to fill the bowls, Sasha said to Charlie, "Tell me the truth, Charlie Barkin. Why did you really come back?"

"It's so heavenly here!" Charlie said, and he kissed her. Everything was fine. Charlie had Sasha. David had his family. Itchy had finally stopped itching. The flying dachshund was happy that all dogs go to heaven too.

Well, not every dog. In a very warm spot very far south of heaven, Carface was learning the hard way that fleas do go to . . . the other place.